Dear Parent:
Your child's love of reading starts here!

Every child learns to read in a different way and at his or her own speed. Some go back and forth between reading levels and read favorite books again and again. Others read through each level in order. You can help your young reader improve and become more confident by encouraging his or her own interests and abilities. From books your child reads with you to the first books he or she reads alone, there are I Can Read Books for every stage of reading:

SHARED READING
Basic language, word repetition, and whimsical illustrations, ideal for sharing with your emergent reader

BEGINNING READING
Short sentences, familiar words, and simple concepts for children eager to read on their own

READING WITH HELP
Engaging stories, longer sentences, and language play for developing readers

READING ALONE
Complex plots, challenging vocabulary, and high-interest topics for the independent reader

ADVANCED READING
Short paragraphs, chapters, and exciting themes for the perfect bridge to chapter books

I Can Read Books have introduced children to the joy of reading since 1957. Featuring award-winning authors and illustrators and a fabulous cast of beloved characters, I Can Read Books set the standard for beginning readers.

A lifetime of discovery begins with the magical words **"I Can Read!"**

Visit www.icanread.com for information
on enriching your child's reading experience.

Library of Congress catalog card number: 2008929406
ISBN 978-0-06-168974-1 (trade bdg.)—ISBN 978-0-06-057415-4 (pbk.)

17 18 SCP 10 9 8 7 6 5 4
❖
First Edition

I Can Read!

BEGINNING 1 READING

The Berenstain Bears'
SLEEPOVER

Jan and Mike Berenstain

HarperCollins*Publishers*

Sister and Brother Bear were having

a sleepover.

Lizzy and Barry Bruin were

Sister's and Brother's best friends.

They were going to spend the night.

Lizzy and Barry's parents brought them
to the Bears' tree house.

"I hope Lizzy and Barry sleep well
tonight," said Mrs. Bruin.

"We'll make sure they don't stay up
too late," said Mama Bear.

Lizzy and Barry put their things
in Sister and Brother's room.
Then they all had dinner.

After dinner the cubs played

a game of Bearopoly.

Lizzy was winning, and soon owned

most of the tree houses.

The other cubs gave up.

Next, they watched a movie.

It was about a wizard.

The wizard had a cape.

It gave him magical powers!

The cubs decided to put on

their own magic show.

They got costumes out of the attic.

The audience was Mama, Papa, and Honey.

The show went well until Barry tripped

on his magic cape.

He knocked over Brother, Sister, and Lizzy!

They laughed and laughed.

"The show is over!" said Mama.

"Time for bed."

The cubs put on their pajamas,
washed up, and brushed their teeth.
Mama and Papa read them
a bedtime story and tucked them in.

"Goodnight, everyone," said Mama,
turning out the lights.

Mama and Papa went to bed

and were soon asleep.

But the cubs were not at all sleepy.

Brother got out his flashlight.

"Let's tell spooky stories!" he said.

Mama woke up.

She thought she heard something.

She woke Papa and they went

to the cubs' room.

Sister and Lizzy were hiding under the covers.

Brother and Barry seemed to be sleeping.

"What is going on here?" asked Papa.
"Brother was telling a spooky story,"
said Sister,
"and Lizzy got scared and yelled."

"That's enough spooky stories," said Mama.
"Now everyone go to sleep!"

Mama and Papa went back to bed.

Mama heard something again.

She woke Papa and they went

downstairs.

They found the cubs in the kitchen
eating snacks.

"It is too late for snacks," Mama said.

"Back to bed!"

Mama and Papa went back to bed again.

But Mama heard a sound in the bathroom.

She woke Papa.

They found Sister and Lizzy
putting on Mama's lipstick.
Brother and Barry were covered in
Papa's shaving cream.
"That's enough of that!" said Mama.
"Back to bed!"

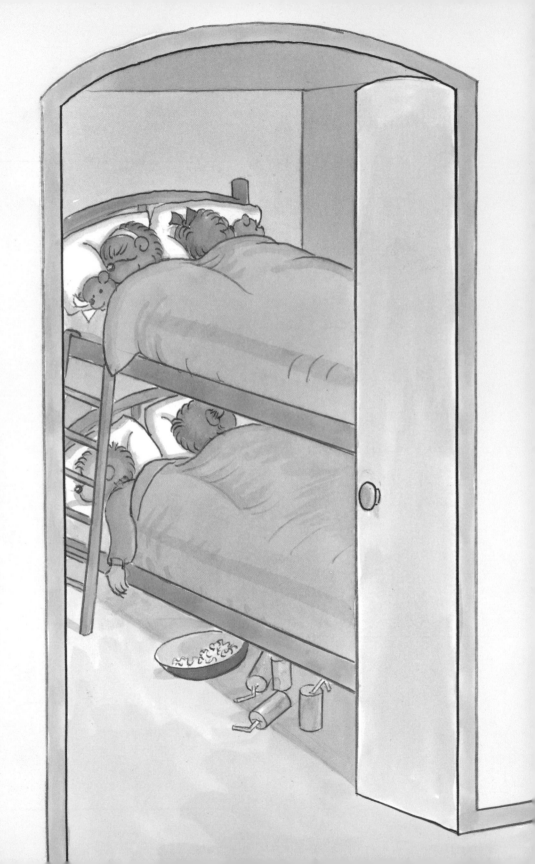

Now the cubs were worn out.

They went right to sleep.

Mama and Papa sat outside

the cubs' room all night.

They did not get much sleep.

The next morning the cubs slept late.

At eleven o'clock, Mr. and Mrs. Bruin
came to pick up Lizzy and Barry.
"I was so worried about them!"
said Mrs. Bruin.
"I didn't sleep a wink all night!"
"Neither did we," said Papa,
his eyes closing.

After Lizzy and Barry went home,

Mama and Papa sat down on the sofa.

They were soon asleep.

It was Mama and Papa's turn for a sleepover!